charcoal boys

roger mello

Originally published as *Carvoeirinhos* by Companhia das Letras, Sao Paolo

First Elsewhere Edition, 2019

Library of Congress Cataloging-in-Publication Data available upon request.

Elsewhere Editions
232 3rd Street #A111
Brooklyn, NY 11215
www.elsewhereeditions.org

Distributed by Penguin Random House
www.penguinrandomhouse.com

This work was made possible by the New York State Council on the Arts with the support of Governor Andrew M. Cuomo and the New York State Legislature.

Archipelago Books also gratefully acknowledges the generous support of the Carl Lesnor Family Foundation, Lannan Foundation, the National Endowment for the Arts, the Ministério da Cultura do Brasil / Fundação Biblioteca Nacional, and the New York City Department of Cultural Affairs.

ART WORKS. National Endowment for the Arts arts.gov NYCulture NEW YORK STATE OF OPPORTUNITY. Council on the Arts MINISTÉRIO DA CULTURA Fundação BIBLIOTECA NACIONAL

PRINTED IN ITALY

for Graça Lima

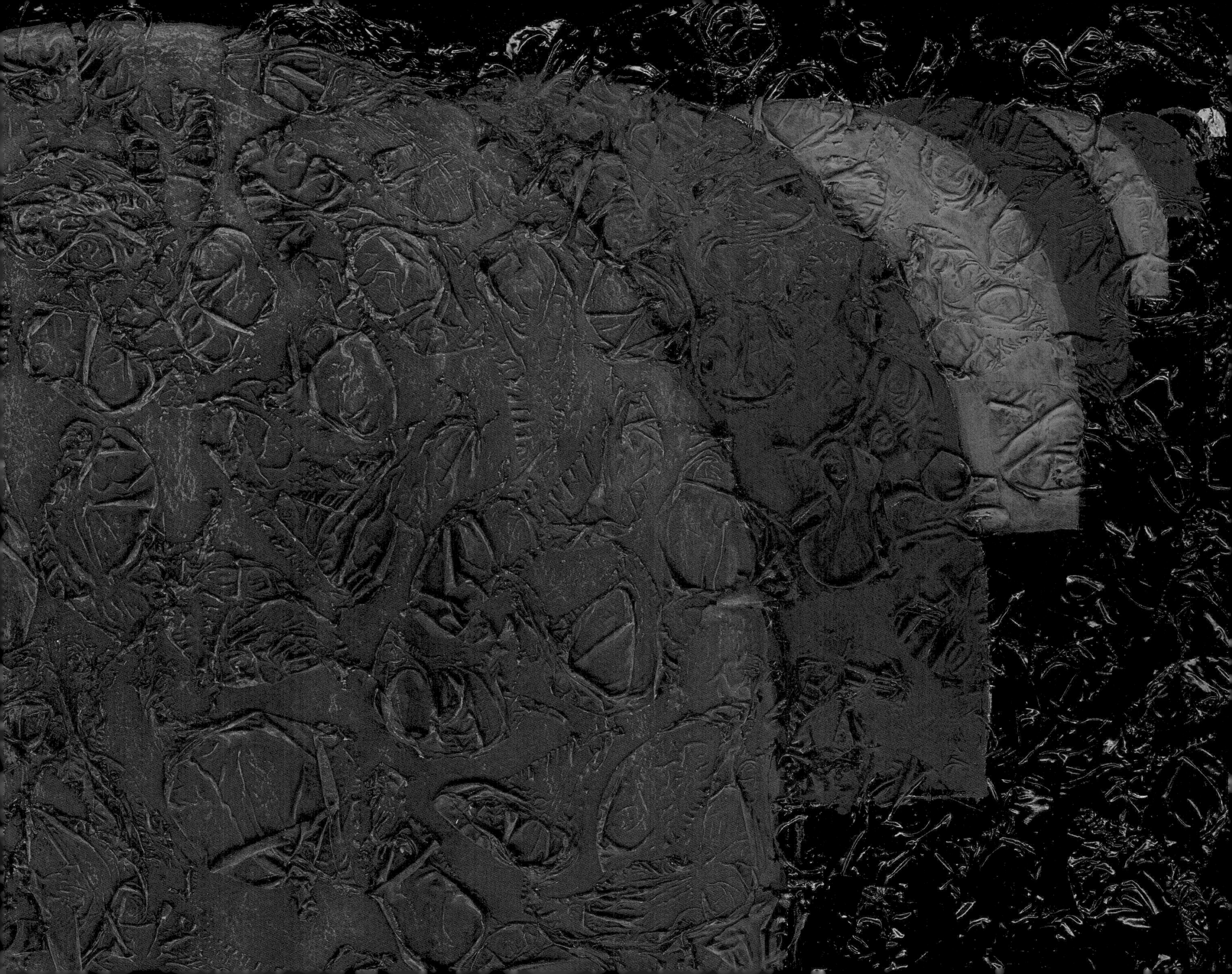

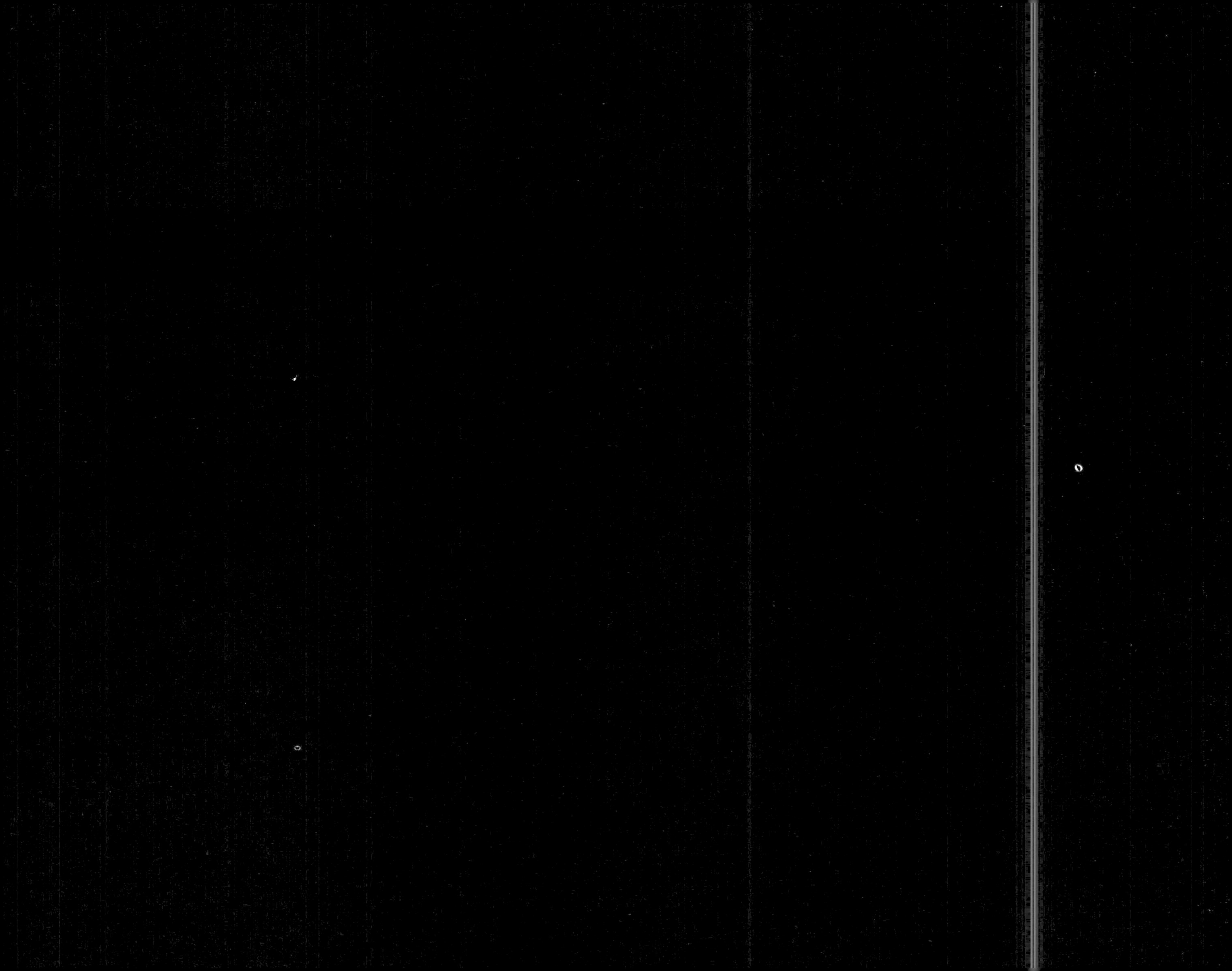

The little coal boys
Pass by on the road into town.
"Hey thar, coalman!"
And they nudge their animals on with a huge horsewhip.

[. . .]

The innocent early hours seem made for them . . .
Tiny, innocent misery!
You dear little coal boys who work as if at play!

"Coal Boys"
Manuel Bandeira
Petrópolis, 1921

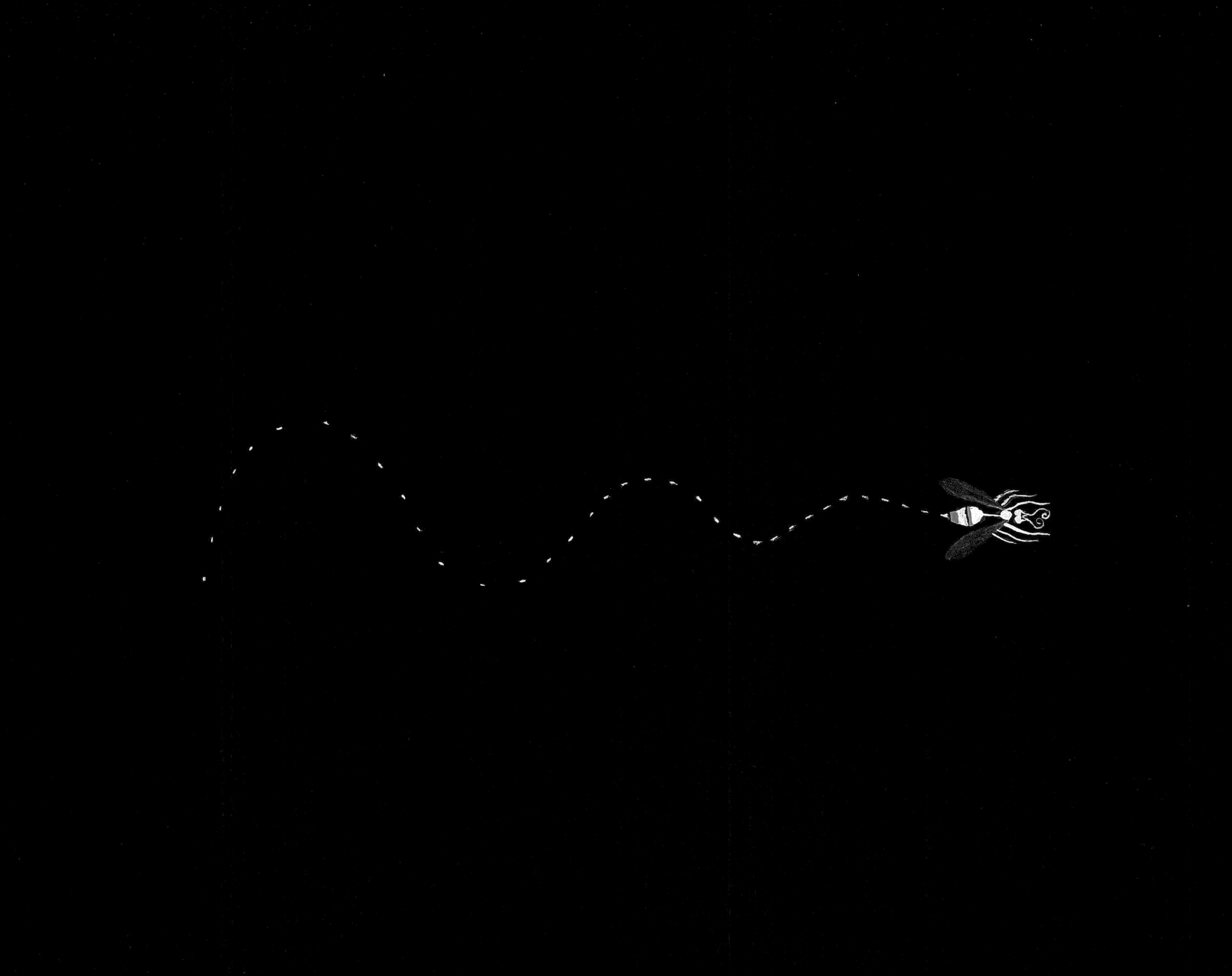

WINGS

Wings know nothing about feet when feet touch the water.

They pretend not to know.

It would be good if that was all, just wings shivering buzzily while wet feet forget about everything. Once they've dried out, wings no longer make any noise. Have I told you that hornet's wings aren't goofy wings like ladybug wings? I have. Nor are they heavy wings like beetle wings, totally useless wings. Or will-they-fall-off wings like a termite's.

Hornet wings are made of wire and tissue paper.

Okay, fine, no they aren't.

I know.

And so they are. Right.

This wing is mine, a hornet's wing, and that is that.

Want to see me change the subject?

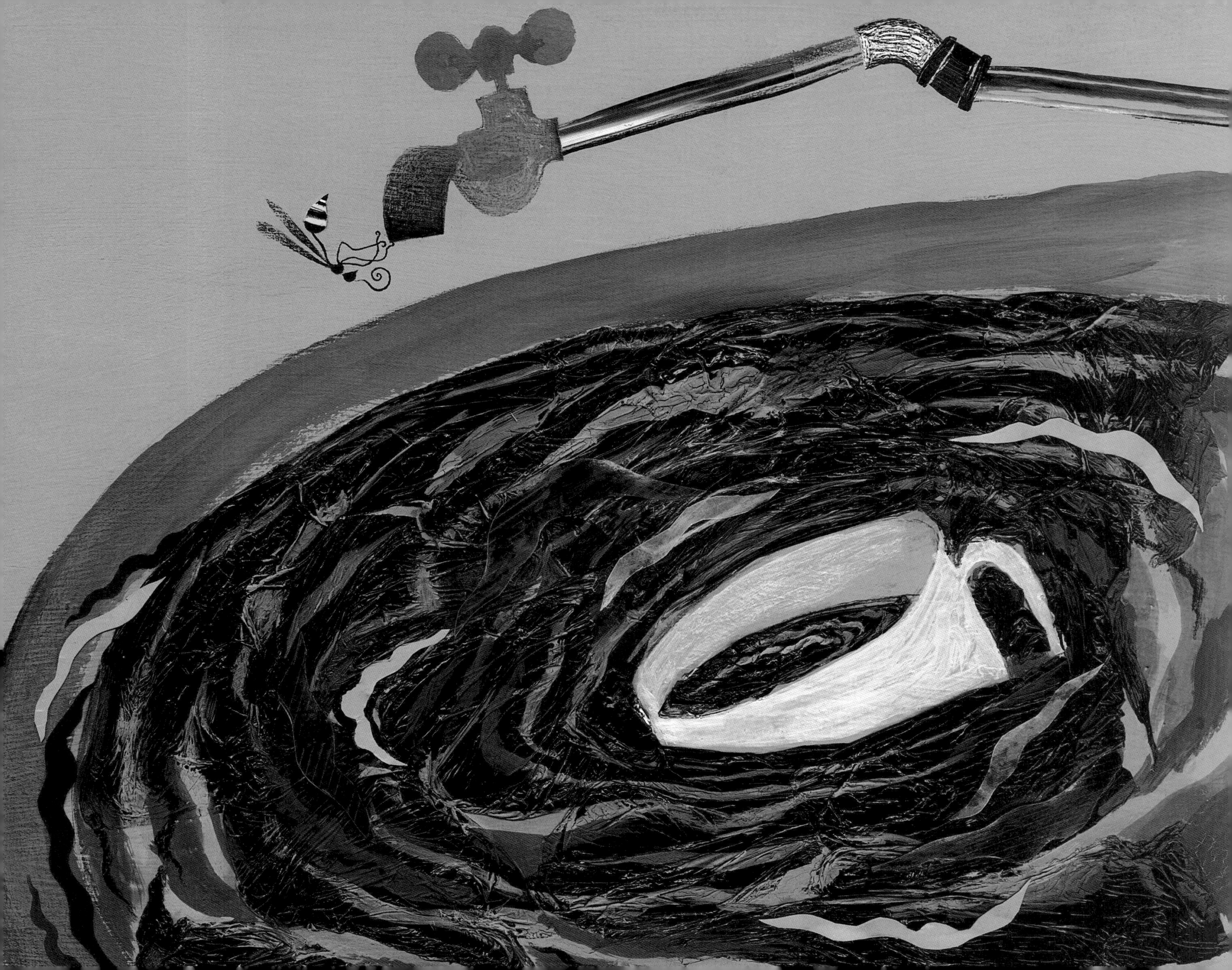

The first time, we met at the big sink for drinking water, me and the boy. He was busy being very thirsty. Him and me. Me and him. I hadn't even unfurled the spiral of my antenna, when that other antenna curled up. The boy pulled the cup out, which was dripping. A brown wave dragged me into the water. Bad luck for me, and I'd only just finished drying my wings. The boy dunked the cup again. Good luck for me. I took advantage of this new wave to cling to the faucet. I tested out a couple of clumsy flights to see if my wings were dry. They were. I made a ball out of a drop of water before it dripped away.

I saw my eye reflected in the ball. In the same ball I saw the boy hurrying off I don't know where, running with the wheelbarrow as if the wheelbarrow was—vroooomm-vrooomm—a Ferrari.

Only later will I understand we aren't so different, the boy and me. We drink water in a hurry to finish a mud house.

The boy's house is not a house. Who said it was? It's a big, round oven.

My house is round, but it's upside-down, stuck to the tile. I created its architecture by spinning a wall around the compass of my body. It's true, I made it out of mud and saliva. My house is not for me. It's a nest where I keep an egg, my hornet boy.

The boy's house is not on its own. A row of other houses that wander off into infinity. It's a house where you put firewood for the firewood to catch fire and then turn into charcoal. The boy's house is not his, it was not he who made it. It is the fire's house. But it is the boy's hand that has just finished the wall, covering up the corners of a hole, mixing mud and a bit of sweat against the side of the oven. Inside, the fire is squeezed, quarrelling with the wet mud and quarrelling with the boy's hand.

Only later will I understand we aren't so alike, me and him. My house keeps an egg, his house embraces the fire.

The boy puts the Ferrari into reverse. He disappears here and there. Other ovens ready sooner are letting out smoke. A row of them—twelve eighteen thirty-two—who can say? I've lost track of the end.

It moved.

Inside my house the egg moved a little. An egg that's hungry.

What can fit into the hunger of a hornet's egg?

I won't tell you now, maybe later.

I take advantage of a gust of warm wind, I get a boost on the breeze. An egg that's hungry . . . where was it I saw a caterpillar again?

In the middle of my search I see the boy and another boy, as white as if he were . . . as if he were . . . my egg. An albino boy and the boy, the two of them talking on a pile of charcoal. One of them is letting smoke out of his nose. The albino boy, I'm gonna call him Albi, Albi is letting smoke out of his nose. A tiniest thread of smoke disappearing into the ovens' great gusts of smoke. They are talking a talk that's funny and full of laughing. Some parts I almost understand:

" . . . and if you sell to the other guys they'll close . . ."

" . . . the coal yard?"

"If you sell charcoal to the other guys they'll close the coal yard."

"No way."

"And if there's a boy . . ."

" . . . they'll close?"

"Even if he's the cook's son."

"Who says?"

"I do."

"What's that?"

"Don't you know?"

"You smoke? Since when?"

"Leave it."

"Give it . . ."

"You can't."

"Give it . . ."

"Like to see you take it!"

You can understand talk like that, coal yard, cook, cigarette. Albi jumped across to the other pile of charcoal, the boy threw himself forward, wanting to get a hold of the cigarette. Then he slipped and went rolling down a short-cut, toppling a heap of bricks.

Didn't I mention? I need a caterpillar to feed my egg.

But all I can see are two boys tangled up.

I need, I need a caterpillar to feed my egg.

Between piles of firewood, I see a boy coughing. A whirlpool throwing up pieces of plastic sheeting pinned down with rocks. I dodge around the whirlpool.

Oof! I need a caterpillar to feed my egg.

The boy went right past Albi, sunk into the charcoal as if forever. Then he jumped totally filthy from one pile to the next, finding his balance in the void. They looked like two lunatics flying, all they needed were hornet's wings.

What I need is a caterpillar. To feed my egg.

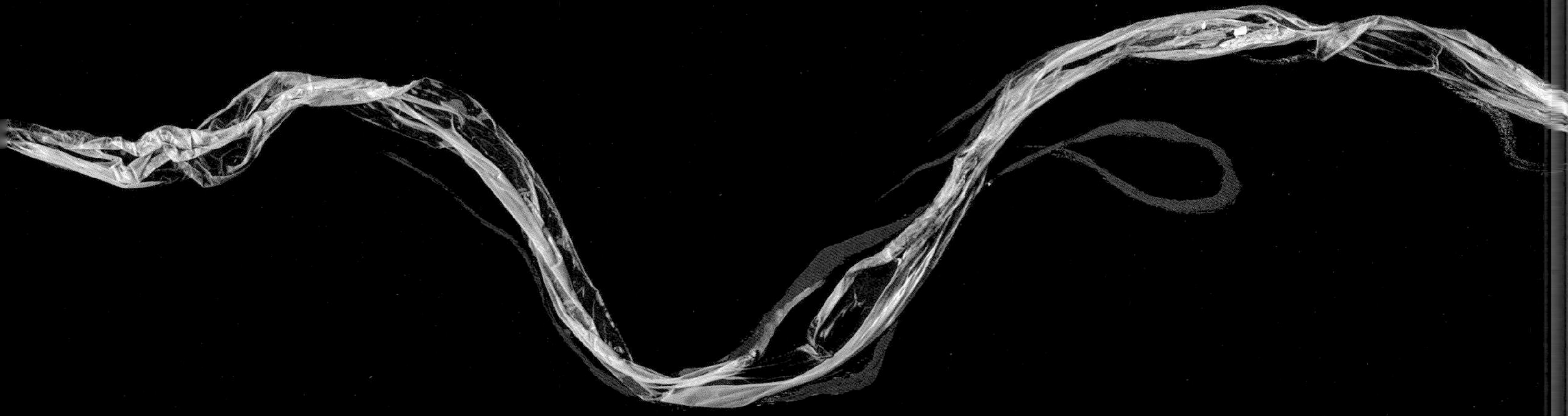

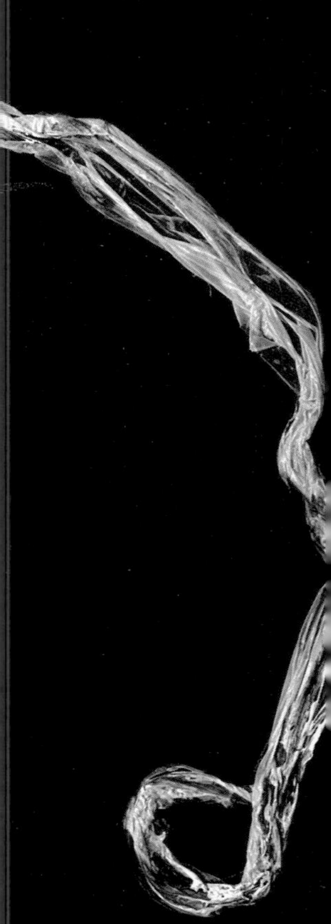

One boy hung on the other's leg, and down they both rolled. Albi's hand swung up. The cigarette flew. The ember from the cigarette came on like a landing light.

A breeze lifts the ember high up.
Look how dry that scrubland is.
Ay-ay-ay . . .

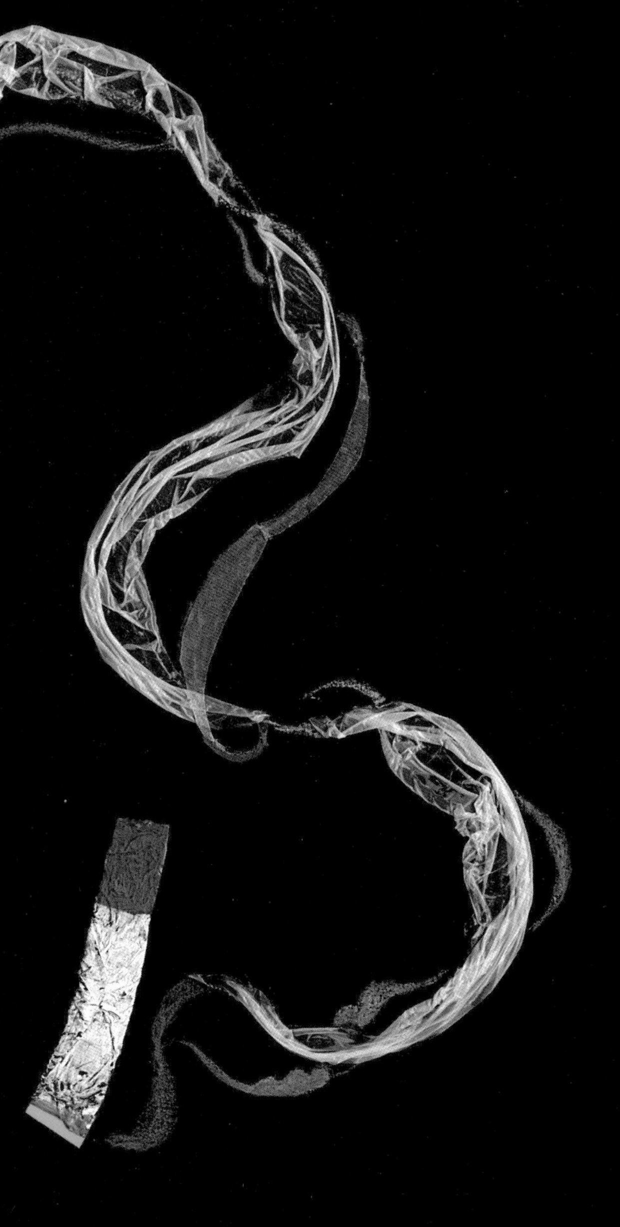

FIRE

I will not talk about the fire.

The fire is nice and big already, he can talk about himself. Ember flame spark, flare flame brazier, tongue, blaze.

An anteater catching fire flees from itself.

Want to know? The fire is nice and big already, he can spread on his own.

The legs of the lapwing look like twigs. They do. Keek-keek. But he doesn't get bothered by his legs, oh no. Keek-keek. He searches for dazed insects in the burned grass and burns his legs in the search. Ay-ay. Take wing, lapwing, it wasn't time to land yet, ay-ay-ay.

After the fire, only the still-hot termite hills catch light. I won't say any more, And now tssssssssssssss.

You won't believe it, but at night the firefly larvae light up the termite hills. The buildings of the termites look like little lit-up cities. Didn't I say you wouldn't believe it?

My egg is crying out with hunger inside the little mud house. A hunger in a hurry. I just needed a caterpillar, but everything's burned now, and soft things like webs, buds, caterpillars, are getting further and further away.

My egg fell asleep hungry.

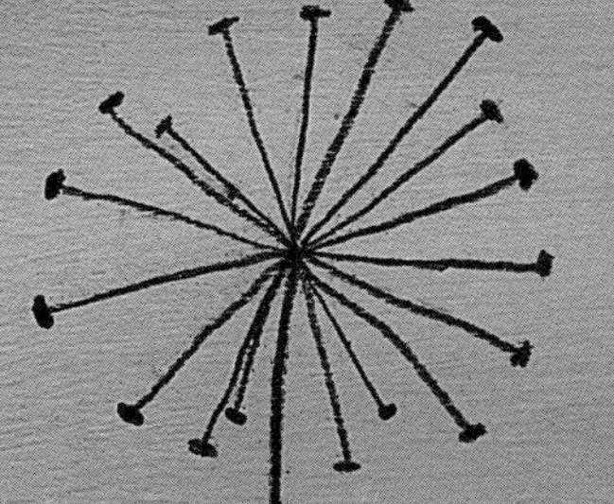

I fell asleep under a real rainstorm. I tried to sleep, wings make a lot of noise once they are wet.

The day startled Albi's house indoors. He pulled aside a sheet of plastic that covered a tile that covered a slit through which he could see the shoes of an inspector here and there crushing the little stones. A good sound like a tire turning a corner on the gravel. The inspection car? This early?

The car door—bam! bam! bam!—made it clear this conversation was not to be heard. Albi quickly put something into his cigarette box and ran out.

Before hiding, he needed to tell the boy. He looked in all the familiar hiding places. What he found was the wheelbarrow carelessly cast aside. Of course: the boy had woken earlier and he was hiding already.

Danger like this demanded a different shelter. He climbed up to the highest point he could think of.

"You hid up here and didn't tell me?"

Where was here? A heap of sacks of charcoal on the back of a truck. Climbing there meant leaning up a ladder, it meant knowing the weight, calculating the fall, the ground, the trouble you'd be in. Albi found the boy, who'd climbed onto the truck without calculating any of it.

"I'll hide here with you."

"Won't work. You show too much."

Albi rubbed charcoal all over his body.

"You still show too much."

He rubbed it again.

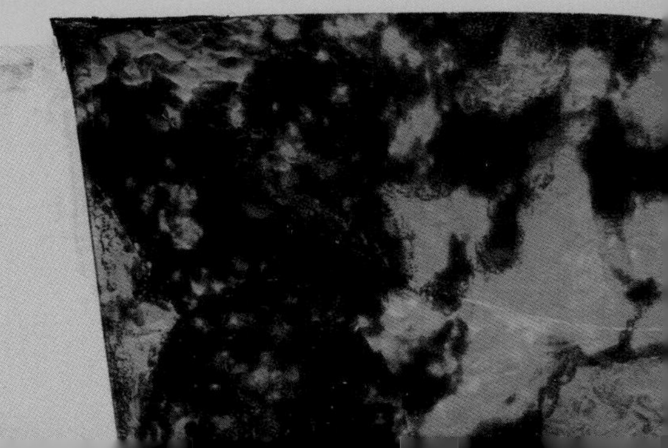

He really did show. The boy didn't. Only his eyes and his teeth, when his eyes and his teeth were speaking:

"Won't work."

"I'm dirtying myself all over."

"Won't work."

He handed the cigarette box to the boy. The boy shook the box beside his ear.

"Is there something inside?"

"Keep it. You can have a look later."

Albi was afraid as he came down from the back of the truck, it was only now he saw the height, those torn sacks spitting out their charcoal were no use for holding on to. He put his weight on the cords, on the edges.

Only when he stepped onto the wheel of the truck did he fall.

"And that boy there?"

He could hear the question the inspector asked from a distance, pointing at Albi's fall.

The foreman of the coal yard looked at him angrily:

"The cook's son."

From way up high, the boy thought he was shuddering, but it was the truck that was shuddering. How was it possible for something so big to move, to turn a corner, to get on the highway? How was it possible?

The landscape was rushing in the opposite direction. If the bed of the truck hadn't been shaking so much, the boy might even have liked the sky before him.

STEEL

A whole day's traveling tying himself to the sacks of charcoal. The boy was deciding when would be the best moment to peek into the box. Not now. Not yet. Best to guess at the inside from outside. A ring? A pencil sharpener? A lucky coin? He didn't even see when the truck skirted the edge of the steelworks.

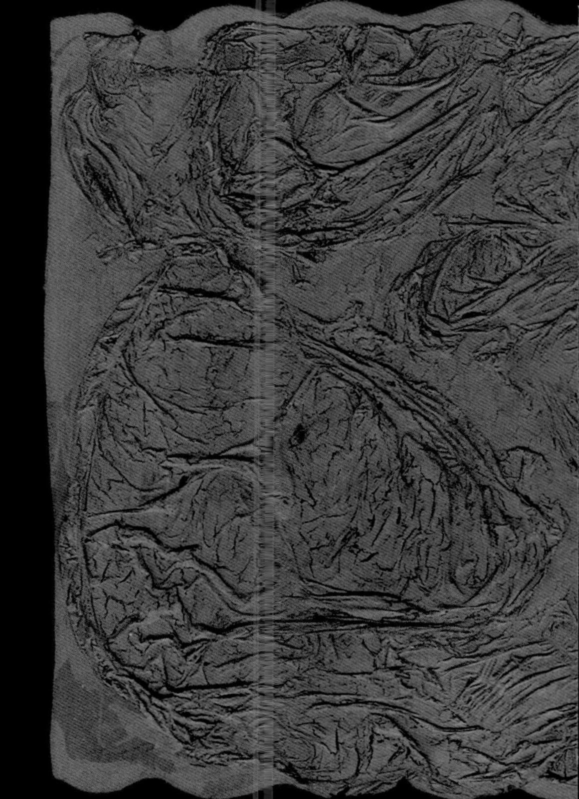

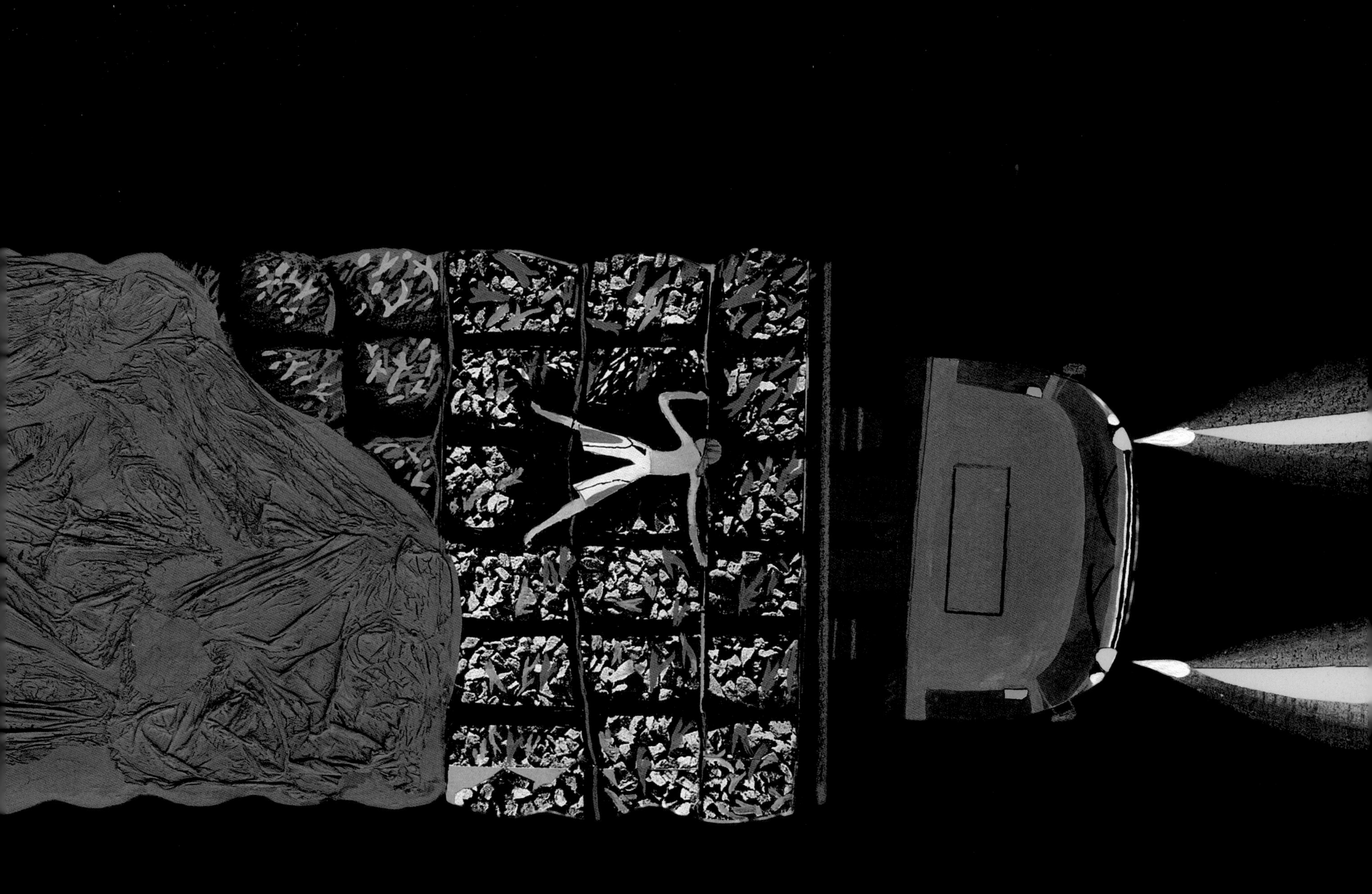

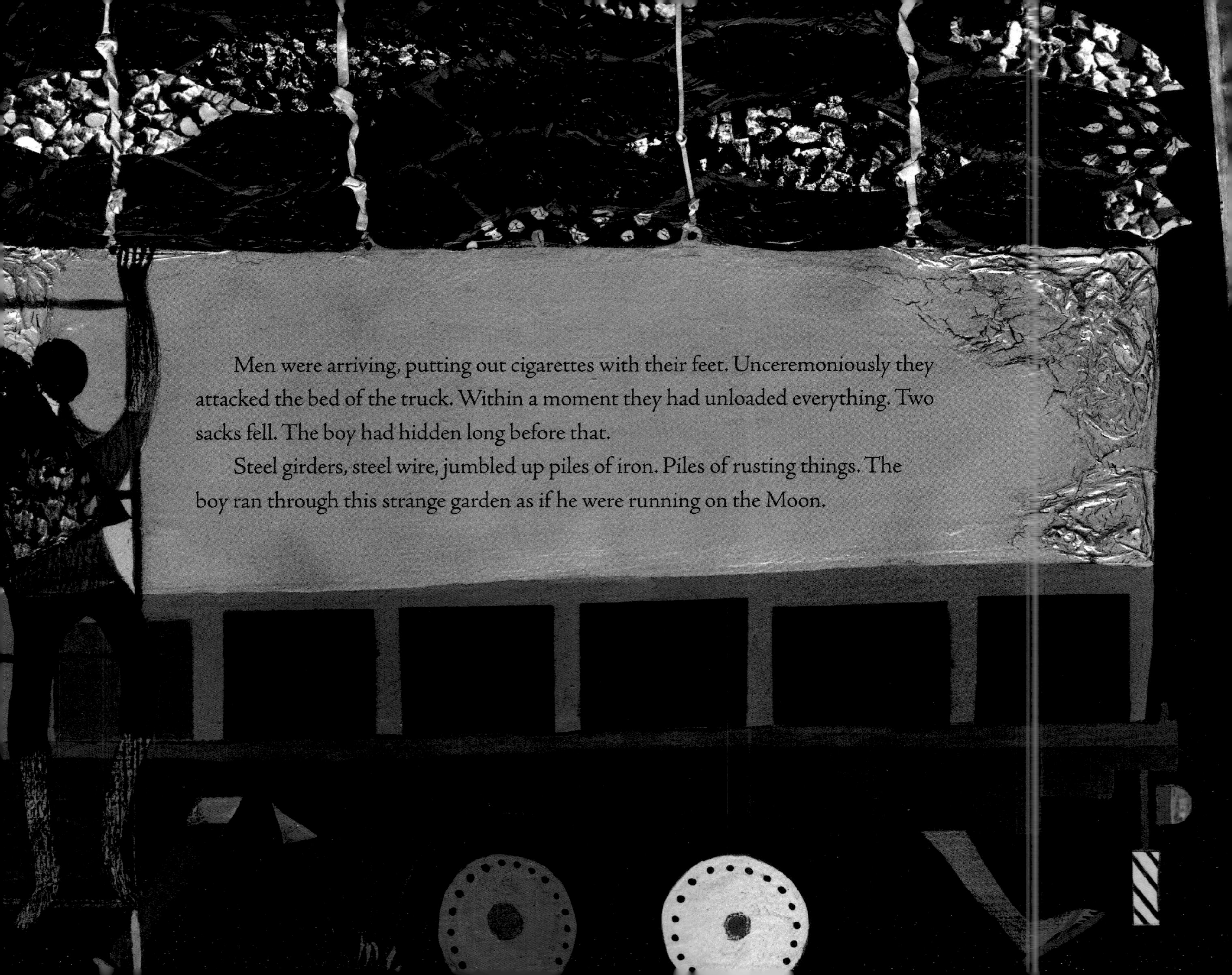

Men were arriving, putting out cigarettes with their feet. Unceremoniously they attacked the bed of the truck. Within a moment they had unloaded everything. Two sacks fell. The boy had hidden long before that.

Steel girders, steel wire, jumbled up piles of iron. Piles of rusting things. The boy ran through this strange garden as if he were running on the Moon.

The world of furnaces is a world made of steel. And yet it's also a world that makes steel. The steel industry is like a huge stomach. The charcoal here dies from all the effort of making the furnaces come alight, while all the ore melts. The blazing iron bars keep on being born.

What is this place? The boy wants to see it from closer up. One of those obsessions they have, all these boys, walking on top of things, balancing on ideas. What they don't have is good wings. Wire and tissue paper. I did tell you. Why is it these people don't fly?

Huge vats were melting iron. How come the vats did not melt? Know what it was that fell out of the boy's hand? A key, from inside the box he was holding so carefully. A key. It disappeared into the furnace.

The truck shuddered that it was time to go back.

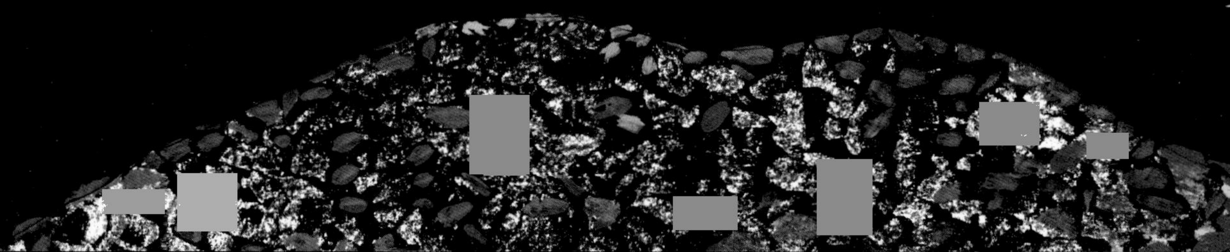

The boy picked up an inchworm and put it in the cigarette box, so the box wouldn't go back empty. The truck that was going back moved apart, the others were going on ahead, laden with steel tubes. Protected by the canvas, from the back of the truck, he saw wagons full to the brim. He saw the railway line biting through the landscape.

All he could think about was the key that had vanished into the furnace.

On the way back, the truck passed the inspection car on the highway. A key. Albi was pressed up against the window. What were Albi and his mom doing in an inspection car? If he could have heard, the boy would have known immediately of the agreement between the inspectors and the man who ran the coal yard. Not even Albi really knew about it. "The key!" Albi shouted soundlessly to him. That part, though, was easy enough to understand. The key. The boy waved goodbye.

When the truck reached the coal yard, it illuminated the wheelbarrow that had been chucked in front of the foreman's house.

I flew over toward the boy. The cigarette box fell. Wow, an inchworm!

My egg would not go to sleep hungry. No, not my egg. My larva.

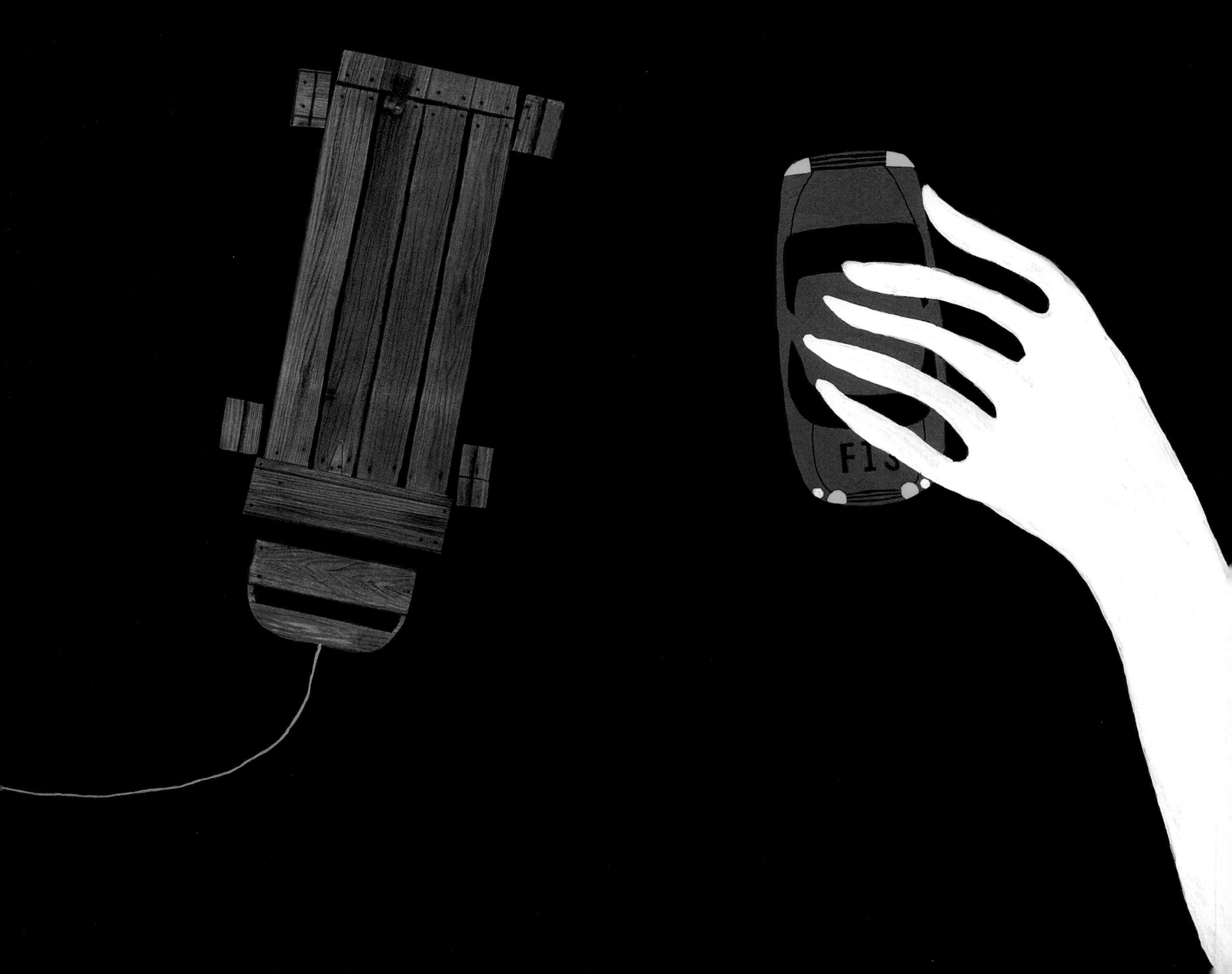

WINGS

Early today I stuck my face outside, the boy had already almost finished blocking up a lit oven.

See: he blocks up about two ovens a day. His hand chooses a brick to close the edges up well, not this one, another, this one, it separates, straightens, it doesn't fit, it makes it fit. It's the hand that chooses. This isn't something the head is needed for, the boy's head is far away. The head is thinking of something else. He turns a brick around, where's it gone? Not this one, not this one, he turns this one here around, I'll split it in half, no not me, he will split it in half, right, that's it, it's the boy's hand that chooses.

Silence, oh…

Any silence is noise, my larva has turned over.

The larva is an ear hearing me.

I give the inchworm to the larva inside the mud house. I put eight small doses of venom on eight points of the inchworm's body. That is so the inchworm doesn't die at once, so it can be food for hornet larva.

Sounds crazy talking like this.

Larva and inchworm are actually quite alike. I'm not gonna explain myself like somebody who says, Oh it's one life for another, the poor little larva needs to feed and to hell with the inchworm. I'm not gonna do that. None of that. It's just really bad. I'm bad.

Bad – me?

It's the boy who's bad. Just look, he's decided to hurl mud to knock down my house.

"It may be a game to you, boy, to me this is an accident, it's a setback, a … Are you listening to me, boy?"

Waste of time, I'm shouting in Hornet, he understands only Boy.

He pays me no attention, however much I . . . however much I shout with my wings. Hornet wings shout, didn't I tell you? Well, no time for these things now. I just have to shout with all the strength in my wings, because a hornet doesn't talk. He only thinks. With all the strength in his bzzz. Flying low is no use at all. The boy laughs. He fans the wind, disturbing my flight. You know what, the wings aren't the only thing in a hornet that shouts. There is something else that shouts louder, funny how people almost always forget about that. But we do use it, though only as a last resort because although the boy doesn't know me, I know him.

There's no other way . . . He's making me do it . . . I'm a hornet, that's just my nature . . . I'm gonna have to . . .

Ay-ay-ay.

Look at the wind dragging me over to the other side as though I were a dead flower!

That's a lie, I'm not dead. A hornet sting isn't like a bee sting, which she uses and then that's that. A meaningless sting.

I know.

A hornet doesn't last forever either.

I won't get to see my son all grown and making his own house beside mine.

But for now it's me, for now it's the wind.

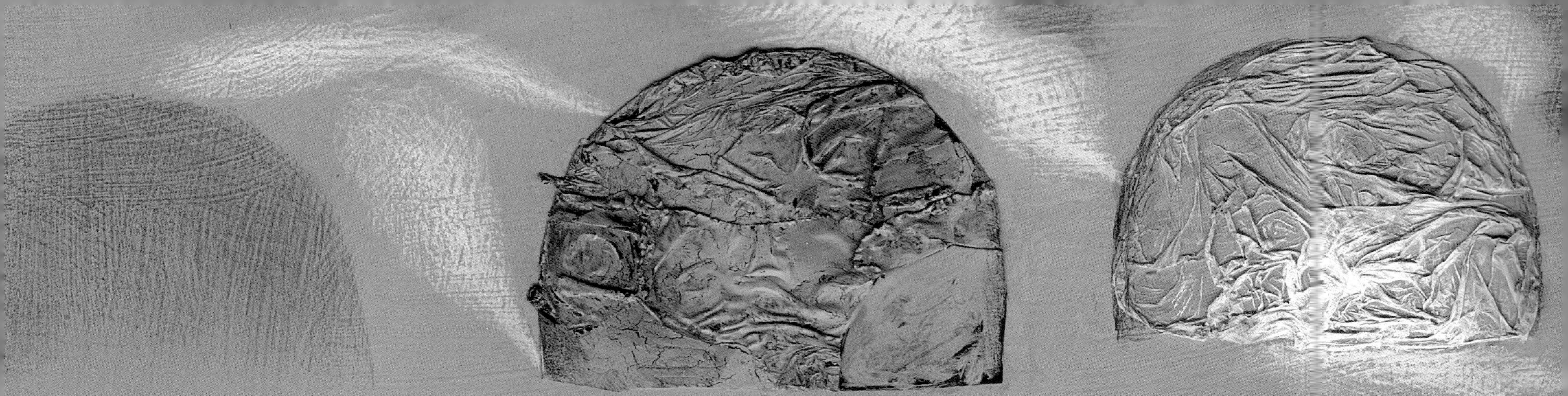

After the sting the boy ran so much, he shouted so much he woke up the whole area. No way to hide a shout as big as the sky. First thing in the morning the inspection car was parked close by. Men laughing and drinking coffee, continuing conversations, their usual thing.

Before getting into the car, two inspectors turned around, the man in charge turned around, the coal yard, the smoke, the sky turned around, the scrubland.

Such a dry shout, who knows why.

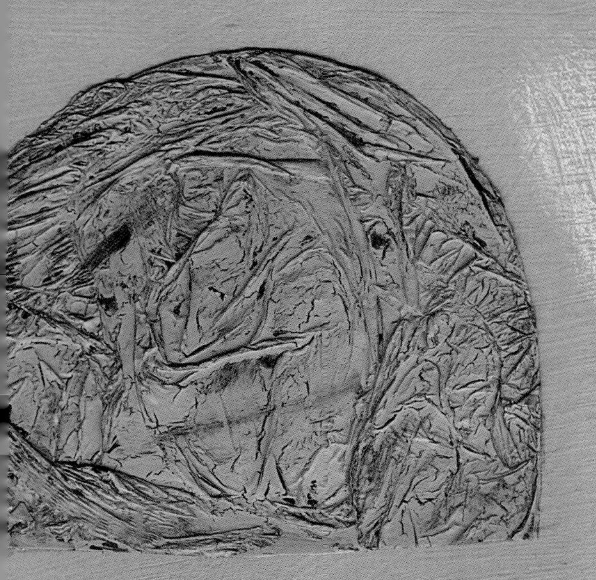

My venom is going wild, it sinks deep. First the boy's finger swells up, it itches, it gets fat.

Before the fever the boy flies . . .

No, not before.

After the fever.

After the fever the boy flies for the first time.

Winner of the 2014 Hans Christian Andersen Award, ROGER MELLO has illustrated over 100 titles – 22 of which he also wrote – and his unique style and adroit sense of color continues to push the boundaries of children's book illustration. Rather than relying on written narrative to tell the story, Mello invites his young readers to fill the gaps with imagination. Mello has won numerous awards for writing and illustrating, including three of IBBY's Luis Jardim Awards, nine Concours Best Illustration Awards, and the Best Children's Book 2002 International Award. In 2018, *You Can't Be Too Careful!* was named a Batchelder Honor Book by the American Library Association.

DANIEL HAHN is the author of a number of works of nonfiction, including *The Tower Menagerie*. He is one of the editors of *The Ultimate Book Guide*, a series of reading guides for children and teenagers. His translation of *The Book of Chameleons* by José Eduardo Agualusa won the Independent Foreign Fiction Prize in 2007 and his translation of Agualusa's *A General Theory of Oblivion* won the 2017 International Dublin Literary Award. He has translated the work of Philippe Claudel, María Dueñas, José Saramago, Eduardo Halfon, and others.

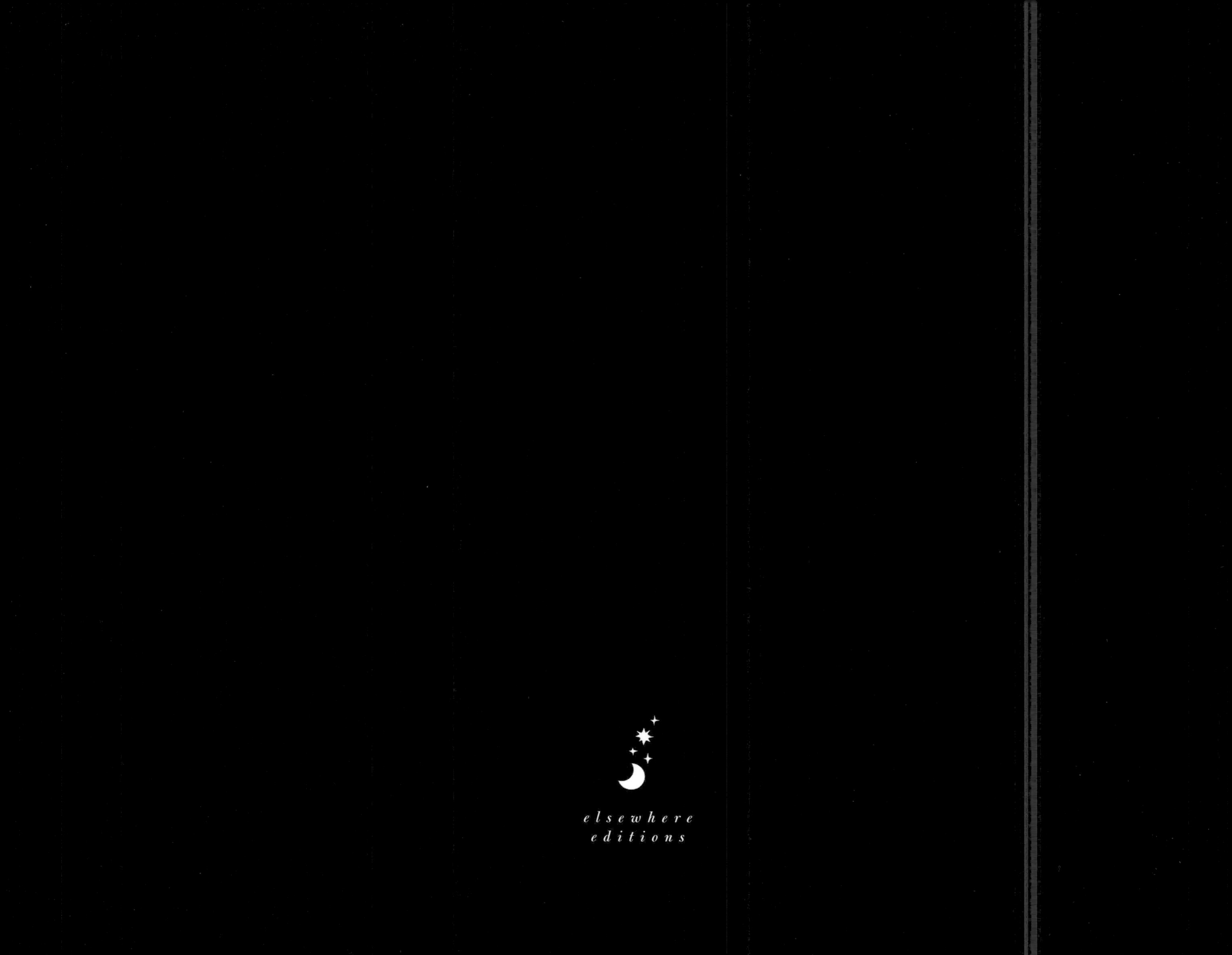
elsewhere
editions